The

DRAGON

NEW YEAR

The DRAGON NEW YEAR

A Chinese Legend

by DAVID BOUCHARD

paintings by ZHONG-YANG HUANG

PEACHTREE

ATLANTA

"Please

do not leave me alone, grandmother! I cannot sleep!"
the small girl cried softly from her bed. "The fireworks
are so bright. And grandmother, why are people
making all that noise?"

Flashes of red, white, and yellow played across her bedroom
wall. From the street below her window came the popping of
firecrackers, the clashing of cymbals, and the shouts and
whistles of people celebrating the new year.

"Do not be afraid, child. It is because of the noise and the
bright lights that we need not fear!"

The old woman sat on the edge of the bed. She smiled,
knowing that, each year at this time, she had told her
granddaughter this very same tale.

"Child. I will tell you the story again, but listen carefully.
Listen and then sleep, so you can wake tomorrow with the
energy every child needs to succeed in a new year.

It is true. Tonight the sky in our village is filled with fiery
lights and deafening noise, but…

Had we been here before, in the olden days, when there were no such
loud sounds or bright lights,...

Had we been here then, we would have found...

Our village so deathly quiet that at midday we could count the mice by the ticking
of their tiny nails on the vacant cobblestone streets.

The school, the shops, and the marketplace would be closed. Every last soul would
have fled to the hills. They would all be hiding from the dreaded New Year.
You understand, child,... that...

New Year is a dragon.

New Year is the most ferocious of all sea dragons. It lives in a palace at the bottom of the sea. Every year it came to our village to satisfy its hunger. Every year, our people fled in fear.

It had been this way for all time, and then one year...

Villagers were feverishly shuttering up their shops, boarding up their homes, and packing enough food to last them through the time the dragon New Year would take to fill its belly. The streets were clogged with people trying to escape.

In the middle of this commotion, a young fisherman was having an exceptionally good day at sea. Times had been difficult because fish had been scarce, but on this day his boat was filled, his nets bulging with every cast he made.

Knowing the time was near for the dragon New Year to feed, the young fisherman scrambled to secure his catch. He set out for the not-so-distant shore. Yet, as time passed, the rocky beach remained distant.

Though he paddled with all his strength, the weight of his cargo and the churning sea prevented him from making any headway. He sat, helpless, on the open water.

It appeared on the crest of a monstrous wave. Hissing and spitting, the
dragon New Year reared its scaly head and arched its long, writhing back.
Slowly, it surveyed the tiny boat. It focused on the young man, crouched
in a corner, frozen with fear.

Lunging forward, in one sweeping mouthful, the dragon scooped up and
devoured the boat, its cargo, and the young fisherman.

Only one person witnessed this tragedy. The young man's mother watched in terror from high on a rocky cliff, where she had gone to hide from the dragon.

As the demon plunged back into the sea, the horrified woman glared at the swirling waters where her son had vanished. She cried out in fury. "Give me back my son! Come back! Give me back my son!" The waters were silent.

The next year passed quickly, and when the anxious villagers made their preparations to flee the coming New Year, the woman went about her daily chores. "Please come with us," they pleaded with her. But in vain. She would stay. She had lost the one person she loved. What had she left to live for? She would stay!

Dusk was falling when she heard a knock at the door. She opened it to find a strange man propped against a gnarled walking stick.

"Have you any food to spare a poor traveller?" he asked, smiling.

Puzzled, she answered, "I have little, but what I have, I will share with you, stranger. But tell me, please, why are you here? Why have you not fled with the others? Do you not know that New Year approaches and this place is not safe?"

"Yes, I know," answered Buddha, for the stranger, unknown to the woman, was indeed the great Buddha.

"I know New Year is coming. But I, like you, lament for my own lost son. So it is that I have come to help you. Listen carefully! This dragon is a sea dragon. It does not know fire! This dragon's home is muffled by the sea. It knows nothing of loud sound! Let us create for it a welcome it will not soon forget!"

"Go!" he urged her. "Go and prepare food for our evening meal out of doors. As you do, find strength through the memory of your lost son. Let the mountains surrounding your village resound with your chopping and beating. Let that sound multiply through the echoes. As for me, I will light a bonfire bright enough to be seen for miles around. This demon of darkness will come to know the power of light and of sound!"

The woman had her doubts, but she did not question her guest. She sensed that she could trust him. Quickly she moved her chopping block outside her house. She gathered her vegetables and what little meat she had, along with the largest of her knives and beaters. Summoning all her strength, she struck and chopped and cut and pounded. The sound echoed through the mountains and spread across the sea in all directions.

As she labored, her strange guest stoked a blazing mountain of fire. He stood, defiantly, waving a flaming branch high in the air above his head. He glowed in the light of the raging inferno.

It came as it had every year. Bursting onto the beach, it slithered with haste toward them.

Fixing them with its cold, snake-like eyes,
its distorted hindlegs dancing in the sand
and its forepaws tearing at the clouds,
the dragon reared to strike.

It reared up. It stopped.

Bewildered, New Year stared at the bonfire.
The flames took on a shape. The shape was
that of a monstrous man—the man who,
as a mortal, had been the young fisherman.

Then, from what seemed like the heart of the mountains came a thundering, frightening clamor unlike anything ever heard at the bottom of the sea. As the woman beat upon her block, the dragon lifted its claws to its head, clutching, frantically trying to muffle the deafening noise.

Its heart pounded as it watched the fisherman of fire whirl around, casting a net of sparks high in the air. The net fell upon New Year, smothering the puzzled beast.

Spitting and hissing, the dragon roared in rage, fighting to escape the web of fire. The fisherman grew ever larger. Slowly he began to haul in his net, lifting the dragon high off the ground.

Kicking and twisting, New Year managed to
free one leg, then another. Still flailing wildly,
like a boulder plummeting from the heavens,
it dropped to the bottom of the sea.

The dragon had disappeared. It had fled,
terrified and confused. And, for the
first time ever, it had left hungry.

This year, New Year would feed in the sea.

Amazed and overjoyed, the woman turned toward her strange guardian. "How can I ever thank you?"

"I have done no more than you would have done for me," he replied modestly. Then, with a gentle smile, he spoke these words: "With your courage and kindness, you have learned to conquer the dragon New Year. You have prepared the way for better and safer years to come. Share this gift as you will."

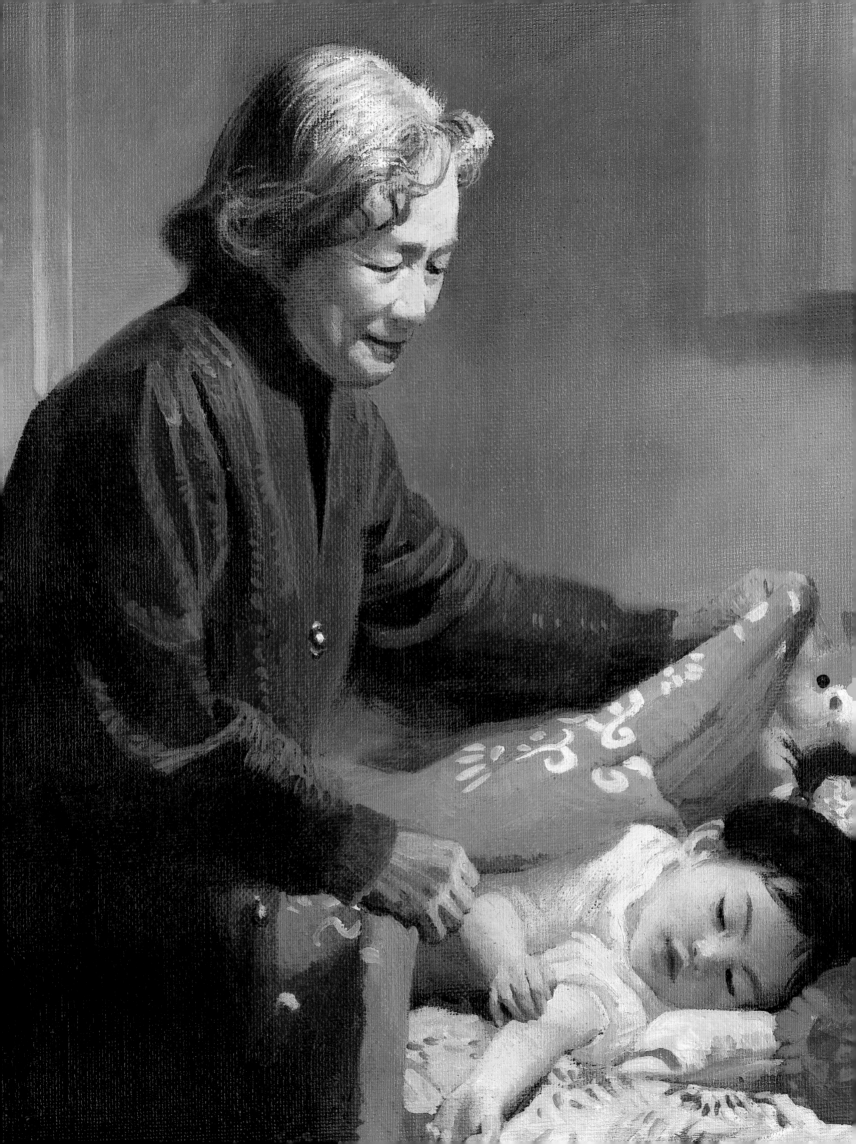

Quietly,

the grandmother rose from the bed. She looked down
at her grandchild, now sleeping peacefully.

She was content, knowing that once again she had shared
this important story—a story that this child would someday
share with her own granddaughter.

And she smiled, knowing that she need not worry about
leaving the child alone in a dark, quiet room…

Because on this night, there would be no darkness…
there would be no quiet…
and…there would be no dragon!

The Buddha,

This just-so story is one way of retelling how the Chinese New Year celebrations came to be, but the real origins of the festival are shrouded in the mists of time.

We do know that the Buddha was a real person, born Siddhartha Gautama, who lived in what is now known as northern India around the sixth century BCE. He was wellborn but abandoned a life of luxury, leaving behind his beloved wife and son, to follow a spiritual path. Historically, there are no records of his having visited China. But the religion he founded, Buddhism, flourished in China in the centuries after his death. There it blended with other religious traditions.

We do know that the dragon of Chinese folklore is a powerful figure, symbolizing strength and good luck. It is perhaps the most dynamic of the animals that are linked to years in the Chinese zodiac. There are dragons of the air, the land, and the sea, with sea dragons being the most secretive. The dragon is an unpredictable creature, who can be a strong and loyal friend, but can just as easily be a mortal enemy.

We do know that the New Year is the most celebrated festival of the Chinese year. According to the Chinese calendar, the New Year begins sometime between mid-January and mid-February in the Western calendar. This is the time of year when Spring first comes to China. Families gather to honor their ancestors and thank the gods for their blessings. The coming of the New Year is celebrated in China and in Chinese communities throughout the world, with much noise and commotion, including parades and fireworks. Some people seal up their doors and windows with red paper to keep out the evil spirits.

WE DO KNOW THAT another tradition of the New Year is the Dragon Dance. A group of people puts on a long, flowing dragon costume made of silk and dances through the streets, gobbling up offerings of money and food through the mouth of the dragon's brightly colored head.

So, IT IS JUST POSSIBLE that, one year, back in the mists of time, the celebration of the Chinese New Year began just as I have told it.

For Jack Wei and the many children who inspire me. — DB

For Sean and Zoe—my dear children. — Z-YH

Published by
PEACHTREE PUBLISHERS, LTD.
494 Armour Circle NE
Atlanta, Georgia 30324

www.peachtree-online.com

Text copyright © 1999 by David Bouchard
Illustrations copyright © 1999 by Zhong-Yang Huang

First published by Raincoast Books, British Columbia, 1999

Printed in Singapore

10 9 8 7 6 5 4 3 2 1
First Edition

Cataloging-in-Publication Data for this book is available from the Library of Congress